Dear Parents:

Congratulations! Your child is taking the first steps on an exciting journey. The destination? Independent reading!

STEP INTO READING® will help your child get there. The program offers five steps to reading success. Each step includes fun stories and colorful art or photographs. In addition to original fiction and books with favorite characters, there are Step into Reading Non-Fiction Readers, Phonics Readers and Boxed Sets, Sticker Readers, and Comic Readers—a complete literacy program with something to interest every child.

Learning to Read, Step by Step!

Ready to Read   Preschool–Kindergarten
• big type and easy words • rhyme and rhythm • picture clues
For children who know the alphabet and are eager to begin reading.

Reading with Help   Preschool–Grade 1
• basic vocabulary • short sentences • simple stories
For children who recognize familiar words and sound out new words with help.

Reading on Your Own   Grades 1–3
• engaging characters • easy-to-follow plots • popular topics
For children who are ready to read on their own.

Reading Paragraphs   Grades 2–3
• challenging vocabulary • short paragraphs • exciting stories
For newly independent readers who read simple sentences with confidence.

Ready for Chapters   Grades 2–4
• chapters • longer paragraphs • full-color art
For children who want to take the plunge into chapter books but still like colorful pictures.

STEP INTO READING® is designed to give every child a successful reading experience. The grade levels are only guides; children will progress through the steps at their own speed, developing confidence in their reading.

Remember, a lifetime love of reading starts with a single step!

Step into Reading, Random House, and the Random House colophon are registered trademarks
of Penguin Random House LLC.

Visit us on the Web!
StepIntoReading.com
randomhousekids.com

Educators and librarians, for a variety of teaching tools, visit us at RHTeachersLibrarians.com

ISBN 978-0-553-53935-6 (trade) — ISBN 978-0-553-53936-3 (lib. bdg.)

Printed in the United States of America

10 9 8 7 6 5 4 3 2

STEP INTO READING®

STEP 1 READY TO READ

nickelodeon

BLAZE AND THE MONSTER MACHINES™

ZEG AND THE EGG

by Mary Tillworth
illustrated by Niki Foley

Random House 🏠 New York

Smash!

Bash!

Crash!

Zeg smashes!

Blaze bashes!

Then Zeg finds an egg.

He does not smash it.

It is a dinosaur egg.
Blaze and Zeg
must return it
to its nest.

Blaze and Zeg drive.

Oh, no!

A big coconut

blocks the road.

Blaze uses a wedge.

The coconut cracks.

Zeg smashes!

Blaze and Zeg go on.

They drive
into a canyon.

Oh, no!

A volcano!

Hot lava

flows into the canyon.

Water will stop
the lava!
Blaze uses his wedge
to crack open
a water barrel!

Water cools the lava.

Blaze and Zeg are safe!

The egg must stay warm.
Zeg wraps the egg
in a blanket.

Crusher grabs
the blanket.
The egg flies up!

It lands

on a mountaintop.

Zeg zooms up
the mountain.
Big rocks fall!

Blaze uses his wedge
to break the rocks.
Smash!
Bash!
Crash!

Zeg and Blaze
save the egg!

Zeg and Blaze
drive to the nest.
The egg hatches!

A baby dinosaur
kisses Zeg.
Hooray for Zeg
and the egg!